AM I
BIGFOOT

by

G.B. Miller

Copywright©2017

The Question, The Conspiracy and The Answer

Writing this story is the last thing I thought I would ever do. Nevertheless, here it is, an apocalyptic, political thriller in three parts staged in the most unlikely place: Reliance, Tennessee. I hope you enjoy it.

Although some of you will see this as a collection of conspiracy theories and others as foolish fantasy, that's okay! For it is, however, just a story. The point is to make you think and then choose.

This is my way of sharing the research of some great men who have inspired me through the years. Men like Ron Wyatt, Kent Hovind, Walt Brown, Ralph Miller, and so many others. I only hope they would approve of the way their theories and findings have been represented.

Thank you for taking the time to find out who Bigfoot is...gbm

TABLE OF CONTENTS

AM I BIGFOOT? 4

TWELVE MONTHS GONE 6

GONE AGAIN 12

ROOM 2021 18

THE STORY 22

THE DEVASTATION 28

GOING TO NOA 35

THE NOAANS.. 41

WHAT THEY KNOW............................... 47

THE WORLD CHANGED 51

HISTORY 56

THE MOVEMENT 62

ROOM 2028.. 69

THE GRAY ROOM 75

THE REST OF THE STORY..................... 81

gbmsound.com

AM I BIGFOOT?

I know what you are thinking. Bigfoot! Really? Yes, I am Bigfoot! I'm also called by many other names like Abominable Snowman, Sasquatch, Yeti, and that crazy guy running around in the woods in a gorilla suit. However, if it's all the same to you, I prefer BIGFOOT!

Most people say I am just a legend, but I don't mind. People love legends. Legends are great! People enjoy telling and listening to stories of legends, especially when they have been *sensationalized*! Nevertheless, most legends are based, in fact, with just a little bit of imagination mixed in.

For example, take the story of the 'Beasts of Givaudan.' These beasts were actually a pack of extremely large dogs, similar to a wolf-mastiff mix. Between 1764 and 1767, they were responsible for 210 attacks with 113 fatalities. The king of France finally had to send his soldiers to kill them. And a couple of generations later, their brutal story had morphed into "The Legend of the Werewolf!"

I, too, have a story to tell! It's not a comedy, a tragedy, a drama, or a historical account. It is, however, all of these.

My story is about a man. A man who had a story of his own to tell. It is funny in places and sad in others, but I must warn you, it's also intense! Therefore, I will only tell you *as much as you are willing to hear...*

TWELVE MONTHS GONE

...Early on a dew-covered spring morning, a very neatly dressed man in his early sixties steps out of the woods in front of the Reliance General Store. The store was the only building at the fork in the road in Reliance, Tennessee, a tiny, rural town at the foot of the Smokies. The store is the grocery, gas station, bait and tackle shop, and post office. In fact, the General Store is the town of Reliance!

The man looked at the store for a minute and then sauntered in and stands perfectly still in the doorway. He was obviously waiting for something to happen!

Noticing the stranger's unusual appearance and behavior, Griff, the rough bearded storekeeper, asked him, "Anythin I can do for ya?" The stranger calmly answers, "May I use your phone, please?" Griff replies, "Sure, no problem...Are ya planning on doin some fishin? The browns have really been tearin it up lately." The stranger shakes his head and says, "No, I just need to make a call." The stranger walks over to the storekeeper. Smiling, he reaches out to shake Griff's hand and says, "Hello, I'm glad to meet you. My name is Gregory...Brian Gregory."

Griff tightly shook Brian's hand, smiling with a toothy grin. Suddenly, with wide-eyed astonishment, Griff blurts out, "Brian Gregory! You're not the same guy that disappeared over there in North Carolina last spring, are you?" Pointing to the other side of the store, he said, "Heck...I have a missing person poster with your picture on it over here in the post office!"

"That's me!" Brian replied with a smile. "May I use your phone now?" Fumbling around for a minute and feeling kind of flustered, Griff said, "Sure...Sorry...But...Where have you been for the past year? Everybody thought you were dead!"

In a thoughtful tone, Brian answered, "I guess I'd better get used to answering that question. I tell you what, as soon as I make my call, I will tell you, *as much as you are willing to hear.*"

Griff reaches into the bib pocket of his liberties and hands over his cell phone. He watches patiently as Brian slowly dials his home phone number. As it rings, Brian's mind races to remember what to tell his wife, Renae, to try to soften the blow. On the fourth ring, a little girl's voice answers, "Hello!" Excitedly Brian asks, "Is this Marie? Uh...may I speak to your grandmother, please?" "Yes it is! And sure you can, just a second. Nonnie, there's a man on the phone for you!" After what seemed like a lifetime, a more serious woman's voice answers, "Hello, may I help you?" "Renae..." Brian said and then paused. Renae immediately recognized his voice, but in disbelief, asked. "Brian?" After another long pause...and in a much quieter voice, almost a whisper, "Brian? I don't understand. What happened to you? Where have you been?"

Fighting back the tears, Brian interrupts to tell her, "I have been in another place...Well, it will take a while to explain. I need you to come here, right now. I am in Reliance, at the general store. Do you know how to get here?" "Yes. I think so," she replied, "I will get Kristine to drive me. I know she knows. We will be there in about an hour...but Brian, what happened?"

 "Trust me, Renae!" Brian pleaded, "I can't tell you just now, but everything will be explained as soon as you get here. Hurry, and be careful. I love you!" Still confused and dazed at the realization that Brian had returned, Renae said, "I love you more!" She hung up the phone and went to get Kristine.

Brian handed the phone back and said, "Griff, would you mind taking my picture with your phone?" Griff said, "Why?" Brian says, "You'll understand soon enough." Brian walked over to the counter, picked up the morning paper, and held it to his chest with the front page facing outward. Griff took his picture and said. "Done! Okay, now let's have it!"

Brian wanted to confirm, so he asks, "Griff, are you sure you want to know? Some things can be hard to hear and even harder to believe." Griff stood up straight as a soldier and said, "Mr. Gregory...I want to know!"

"Very well!" Brian said as he and Griff walked over and sat down in the store's barrel chairs beside the checkers' table. Everything got very still until the only thing you could hear was the pump running in the minnow tank. Brian looked Griff directly in the eyes and said, "What do you know about Bigfoot?"

When Griff heard this, he jumped up and shouted, "BIGFOOT! You're not gonna tell me that you spent the whole year hanging out with Bigfoot? Where did you sleep? In his cave?" Brian leaned back in his chair and calmly said, "Yes...and No. What if I told you Bigfoot is not a Bigfoot? What if I told you, Bigfoot is not what people say he is?"

"Bull!" Griff barked, "Then tell me this, if Bigfoot really did exist and is not an animal, what is he? Mister, I have lived, fished, and hunted in these mountains my whole life, and if there was a Bigfoot, I would've seen him by now! Every yokel I've ever known, who saw a Bigfoot, was a liar, crazy or drunk at the time. I'm just trying to figure out which one you are. Don't get me wrong, I don't think you're a liar, and it's too early to be drunk."

"Maybe I'm crazy!" Brian mused, "And you did say you wanted to hear my story." "Whatever," Griff mumbled. Brian continued, "All I'm trying to tell you is where I've been and how I got here today!" Brian pointed out, "I guess that the only evidence that I am still alive is that picture. As a matter of fact, you're the first person to see me in twelve months!"

Griff sat back down, shook his head, and said, "Mr. Gregory, I'm sorry. It's just that I've heard these stories for years, and never has one had any credibility at all. What makes yours' any different?"

"Griff," said Brian kindly, "What if the story I tell you isn't true? It wouldn't cost you anything but time. However, if my story is true. You would have to decide if you really want to know. Because knowing may change your life!

I didn't ask for what happened to me, but I am glad that it did. Even if the price I had to pay would be losing everything I love most in the world! Sometimes you have to lose something to save it. Now, do you want me to continue or not?" "I guess so." Griff said.

So starting with last April, Brian described in detail all of the events of the past twelve months. When Brian had finished, Griff sat there dumbfounded. When he came to himself, he just said, "WOW! For the first time in my life, this all makes sense. But, you gotta know there's a lot of folks who wouldn't want this to get out! Aren't you putting yourself in danger?" "Maybe." Brian said, "But this was my choice.

Nevertheless, what we have to do now is going to be the most critical part. Making sure my family understands why I am going to do what I must do next. I have to take this information to some people who may not listen. My commission is to take this message to the people who fear this truth the most."

Just then, they heard someone pulling up in the gravel outside. "Your wife must be here," Griff noted. "She made good time!" Brian and Griff made their way to the front door. However, as they stepped outside, twelve men in suits were getting out of three black SUVs.

GONE AGAIN

Griff exclaimed, "This ain't good!" Immediately Brian told him, "Griff, don't let on that you know anything. You have to explain everything to Renae and Kristine when they get here. For now, just play dumb!" Griff acknowledged with a subtle nod.

Then he turned towards the men and welcomed them with a smile, saying, "Howdy! You gentlemen commin up for the trout fishin too, or just getting away from the city for a while?"

However, the men totally ignored Griff. They were all staring at Brian! The man in charge said, "Mr. Gregory, we have a few questions for you. Please come with us."

The last thing Griff saw of Brian was him being frisked and then trundled into the middle SUV. They whipped around out of the parking lot and disappeared in a cloud of dust down the two-lane country road towards Benton.

Griff just stood there numb. In the past hour, he had seen and learned more than he had his whole life. Reliance had always been a quiet, peaceful place to fish and get away from it all. Excitement is just not done here!

About five minutes later, as he waited on the stoop, he saw Renae and Kristine pulling up in the lot. Griff walked out to meet them but stopped just short of the pumps. As they got out of the car, he said, "Renae, my name is Griff Miller. Brian asked me to give you a message just before he was taken." Renae stopped dead in her tracks, her excitement disappeared, and her expression turned to that of hurt and confusion.

Griff seeing their pain, said with a comforting voice, "Come on inside...We need to talk." They followed Griff inside and sat down in stunned silence as he poured them a cup of coffee. Griff sat down across from them, and as if he were a master storyteller, he started laying out everything just as Brian had told him.

"Renae, the first thing Brian wanted you to know is that it was not his choice to leave you and the kids last spring. Brian is being led down a long and challenging road, which many people have had to walk before. He told me of the events which brought him to be where he is now. Although he wasn't able to tell me everything, I will tell you what I know. I will tell you *as much as you are willing to hear*.

As you know, Brian went with Walter, Ronnie, and some of their friends to the Bigfoot Watch &

Campout on the North Carolina side of the Smoky Mountains last April. Although Brian did not believe that Bigfoot existed, he went along just to spend time with his old friends.

On the evening of the sixth, about 9:30pm, Brian walked out into the woods to relieve himself. He was not seen or heard from again until today. His friends and the authorities searched for months, but they assumed a bear or some other wild animal killed him after finding several huge and strange tracks in the area.

However, totally unknown to his friends, there was an actual 'Bigfoot' prowling around, listening to them. He was searching for a suitable candidate to abduct. This particular Bigfoot had been conducting a search, which had lasted many years. Finally, he found Brian, who fit his profile perfectly. Brian was abducted and taken to a place where he was trained to be a messenger."

Kristine suddenly jumped up and started pelting Griff with questions. "Bigfoot? Where did Bigfoot take my dad? What kind of a messenger are you talking about? And who was it that took him just now?" Griff held up both hands in a calm down gesture, and he continued.

"According to Brian, what we call a Bigfoot is not an animal at all. The few genuine images we have seen of Bigfoot were secretly posed by the

Bigfoots themselves! This is their way of getting people to search for the mythological creature in an environment where they can evaluate and classify us without exposing themselves. The hairy appearance we've all seen is simply a type of camouflage.

The creatures known as Bigfoot are completely human. Actually, they are more human than we are. They call themselves Noaans, and for many thousands of years, have had an advanced civilization far below our own in enormous chambers left behind by a global devastation.

They chose Brian and several others from all over the world and took them to their underground home to be trained as messengers. Brian said the lessons they have learned consisted of universal history, extremely advanced science, as well as the current social and political environments. Everything they would need to complete their missions. The Noaans have been training messengers for thousands of years."

Renae interrupts, "Do you mean they have been controlling the human race all this time?" Griff said, "No. Oh no...The messengers are thoroughly trained and then sent out just to help us better understand the overall plan. However, we have always had the freedom to choose our own way.

According to the Noaans, people were designed to be so much more than we see today. In fact, they told Brian that we actually are Noaans! However, due to the precautions that they took immediately following the devastation, they more closely resemble the original design than we do. Nevertheless, even with these precautions, they too have been degraded far from the original Noaans."

Finally, he summarized the most crucial part of Brian's message by telling them, "Brian told me that we are a short time from the seventh millennium. Brian was tasked with taking the only solution, to the few who will listen, in the midst of those who will not. And the ones who listen to him will take it to those who will listen to them."

When Griff finished telling the story, they all sat quietly for a few minutes, trying to absorb it all. Griff broke the silence and said, "Ya know, I think Brian knew that I would be here to listen to his story, so I could tell you guys. And...Now that I think about it, all this must be part of some kind of elaborate plan! Brian knew that these government guys were looking for him, and they were listening in for his call. I also think that everything he did was to prepare us for this message and to set the necessary events in motion." As Renae and Kristine listened intently, Griff continued to detail all he could remember. Griff suddenly felt he must do what he can to help Brian complete his mission as he was speaking.

Renae said, "I love Brian, he's a kind and intelligent man, but he is not smart enough to come up with this!" "Is anybody?" questioned Kristine. "No!" said Griff. "This plan is far too complicated and has been going on too long for Brian, or even the Noaans to have dreamed it up. There is a level of detailed organization to these events we cannot understand or imagine. What's more, I am sure Brian told me the story because he wants me to help spread it too.

And I think I know how to start. I will get some of those news guys to come up here to cover a story about another 'Bigfoot sighting in the

Smokies'. They love that kind of stuff. I reckon folks will think I'm just another crazy wacko, but I don't care; the story will eventually get out.

As for you guys, tell your family and friends, but be careful. Sooner or later, this will get out, and we don't know what to expect. Nevertheless, Brian is doing his part, God help him, and we should do ours." Griff stands again, thinking aloud, "Lord only knows where he is now!"

ROOM 2021

As Griff was telling the story, Brian was sitting quietly in the back seat of the center vehicle, flanked by agents. The caravan of black SUVs made the ninety-degree right turn onto highway 411, heading north towards Knoxville.

After about twenty minutes, Brian spoke out, "Agent Cartwright...How much longer to Oak Ridge?" In a gruff voice, Agent Cartwright barks, "How do you know my name? And what makes you think we're going to Oak Ridge?" Brian calmly replies, "Because we are."

Suddenly the agent to Brian's left very roughly says, "No more talking!" Brian tells him, "Okay, Rocky." The agent's eyes widened, and his face turned as white as a sheet as he stared at Brian in shock. Irritated to no end, Agent Cartwright shouts, "Who the hell is Rocky?" The agent in the backseat murmurs, "My grandfather used to call me Rocky." Everyone was quiet for the remainder of the trip.

About an hour later, they passed through the security gates at the Oak Ridge Nuclear Research Facility. The rest of the caravan continued forward, down the road towards the main facility. However, the SUV containing Brian peeled off to a side street and entered an underground bunker, parking in front of a loading dock.

A half-dozen armed marines quickly surrounded the SUV. As everyone got out, Brian was greeted by an older, gray-haired gentleman. He was very official-looking. He pointed towards a door beside the loading dock and said, "This way, please."

They all proceeded through a dark corridor, which looked like it was fashioned from a twelve-foot, corrugated steel drainage pipe and into a complicated maze of rooms and hallways. As soon as they got into this area, the marine escort stopped, turned around, and disappeared back down the corridor. Only Brian, the agents, and the older gentleman seemed to be in the bunker or at least the main hallway.

Brian was shown into the fourth room on the left side of the hallway, room 2021. Upon entering, he noticed a one-way mirror and seven cameras strategically placed throughout the room. The room was very comfortably decorated with pictures, couches, chairs, lamps, coffee tables, and a wet bar in the corner.

The older gentleman pointed to an armchair and said to Brian, "Make yourself comfortable." As he settled down into the chair, Brian said politely, "Thank You" The older man said, "My name is Mr.

Baker, and I guess you wonder what you are doing here." Without hesitation, Brian answered. "Not really…Mr. Brooks."

With a very impressed look on his face, Mr. Brooks said, "I guess you know quite a bit about us as well! Therefore, I can assume that you know what we want to know." "Of course." Brian stated, "You want to know what I know." "Indeed!" said Mr. Brooks.

Brian said, "Today, I will tell you the whole story of where we've come from, where we are in history, where we are heading, and of course where I've been the past twelve months.

You may believe me, and you may not. However, truth is not always what we want it to be. Truth is what it is! What's more, the things I have seen and heard over the past twelve months may be difficult for you to swallow, so I will only tell you, *as much as you are willing to hear*!"

"That's all we ask," said Mr. Brooks. "Very well," said Brian, as he pushed back into the plush armchair and prepared to lay out a comprehensive account of his fantastic adventure.

Brian glanced around the room at Mr. Brooks, Agent Cartwright, and the three other agents lounging in the other chairs. Brian smiled a friendly smile and said, "I will tell you my story and answer your questions as best as I can. However, I will only talk as long as you are willing to listen." Mr. Brooks nods in affirmation.

"Thank you." Brian said, and he continued, "I will tell you about my capture first, about the people who abducted me, and finally the message. You may ask questions at any time during this process. However, I have not come here to argue or debate. Therefore, I will answer only one question at a time and only from someone physically in the room…No ghost over the intercom, no prepared list, and no one-way conversations!" Is this format acceptable to you?"

They looked around the room at each other for a second, and then Mr. Brooks replied, "Yes, we accept your terms." Everyone was in agreement, so they sat back and listened intently as Brian begins to tell his story.

THE STORY

Brian starts, "One year ago today, I was camping with friends in the North Carolina side of the Cherokee National Forest, north of the Hiawassee River Campground. We had spent the day fishing and hiking, which by the way, is not my favorite pastime. On April sixth at approximately 9:35pm Eastern Standard Time, I felt the call of nature, so I walked about fifty feet down the path, southeast of the camp, to relieve myself...number one.

As I was doing my business, I could hear the voices and laughter very clearly coming from the camp. Especially Ron and Walter, who are notorious cut-ups! I digress. Upon finishing my business, I turned around and bumped into what I thought was a tree. I remember thinking that I didn't notice a tree being there before."

Agent Cartwright spoke up, "Did you hear any movement in the woods behind you? And had you been drinking alcohol, or maybe taking any drugs which may have impaired your ability to perceive your surroundings?"

Brian noted, "That's two questions! However, the answers are...no and no. Even so, I had no idea anything moved so quickly and quietly that it could come up behind me, under clear skies with moonlight, in dry woods without being detected audibly or visually. Still, I turned and walked into the object, which I assumed to be a tree. A little stunned, I stepped back and then looked up into a small cloud of sweet-smelling mist. The last thing I remember is seeing two eyes looking down at me.

Later, when I woke up, I saw a young man standing beside me, smiling. I was lying on a bed in what I thought was some medical facility. As my head started to clear up and I became more aware of my surroundings, I realized this young man had to be almost nine feet tall. At first, I freaked out. I thought I must be dreaming...or dead!"

"Almost nine feet tall?" Mr. Brooks exclaimed, "How could that be?" Amused by his apparent confusion, Brian smiled and said, "I thought the very same thing to myself. THIS IS IMPOSSIBLE! However, there he was, there I was, wherever 'there' was, and all I could do is try not to freak out long enough to figure out what in the world was going on!"

Mr. Brooks pipes up again, "Surely you don't expect us to believe that there is a race of people almost nine feet tall?" Smiling, Brian replied, "Of course not. As it turns out, Sada-BarSet, the young man who captured me, was short for his age, only 8'-11" tall. The current overall average height of an adult Noaan, that's what they call themselves, is about 11'-9" tall."

"What a crock!" Brian heard one of the other agents say. "And why is it a crock?" Brian queried. "Have you ever met a Noaan?" The agent responded quickly, "Everyone knows that the average person is taller today than people were, even one hundred years ago, and nobody is eleven feet tall!" Brian touted. "Really! Who told you that?"

Brian started laying it on thicker. "Who is everyone? Scientists, anthropologists, teachers, and professors in our government school system?

As you know, thirty years ago in the USSR, everyone taught that communism was the best form of government, and if they disagreed, they were taken for an extended vacation in sunny Siberia! Most teachers teach what they are told to teach, or they are banished to academic Siberia. Teachers who teach any theory about life's origins other than evolution know that they could face disciplinary action and/or termination.

Furthermore, most scientists and anthropologists have totally ignored or even hidden the fact that numerous skeletal remains of humans, approximately twelve feet tall, are found all over the world! These are remains of ancient Noaans, who had come to the surface for one reason or another. Of course, the evidence has been stashed away in the basement of the Smithsonian and other institutions of higher learning for safekeeping. The Smithsonian even has a nickname for them, The Army of the Potomac!"

Additionally, there is an incorrect worldview being taught by most of our teachers and professors, which even they are not allowed to question! And when your children enter a government school, they are shown many textbooks with multiple references to Millions of Years Ago!

What's more, despite the lack of evidence for this theory, it's consistently taught and becomes most students' worldview. This is not education. It is, however, indoctrination!   For years, your government has been teaching its religion to your children in schools funded by your taxes.

Agent Cartwright spoke up, "What about those remains you mentioned? If they have been hidden away from the public, how do you know about them?" Brian promptly answered, "The same way I knew your name, Special Agent Dave Cartwright. Oh, by the way, there is a lot more to this story, so you had better call your wife Carrol to let her know you'll be late for supper."

Suddenly, the room grew deathly quiet until the muted sound of someone gasping and dropping their ink pen was audible through the glass from the control room. Now, there was a thick cloud of tension in the air!

To lighten things up a bit, Brian said, "I'm parched...Do you think I could get a glass of water?" Mr. Brooks stood up, went over, and opened the small fridge under the bar. "Would anyone else like a bottle of water?" he said. No one else wanted one, so he took one for himself and gave one to Brian. "Thanks!" Brian said.

Mr. Brooks noted, "You are very polite. You have obviously been taught good manners. Was this part of your training by the Noaans?" "Thanks again!" Brian smiled as he replied, "But no. My parents taught me good manners from a very young age...It was not optional!" Mr. Brooks chuckled. "I know what you mean. Please, continue."

However, before Brian could speak, Agent Jones (Rocky), the agent from the car, asked, "How did they get so tall?" "Good question!" Brian answered, "They didn't. The correct question would be, 'How did we get so small'?

Choices! It all came down to the choices made by ourselves and our ancestors." The agents were on the edge of their seats as Brian elaborated, "Thousands of years ago there was what the Noaans refer to as 'The Devastation.'" "What kind of devastation was it?" Agent Cartwright asked. "I was just coming to that," Said Brian, then he continued with his story.

THE DEVASTATION

"The Devastation was a cataclysmic event which fundamentally changed the environment of the entire planet. It destroyed a protective barrier, made of ice, suspended above the atmosphere. This ice barrier was held in place by three major forces. The earth's atmospheric pressure, the vacuum of space, and the earth's gravimetric field. The barrier's demolition has reduced the atmospheric pressure by almost half through the centuries and the oxygen levels by one-third. The barrier's collapse also allowed the sun's harmful x-ray and gamma rays to penetrate the atmosphere, which they could not do before.

Furthermore, the destruction of this barrier caused most of the barrier's ice material to explode outward into space because of the pressure differences. Resulting in large portions of this minus four-hundred-degree ice, because of its static charge and the earth's gravity, being drawn back down, mainly towards the earth's magnetic poles. This caused what we now call the Ice Age.

To make things worse, enormous ice meteors penetrated the atmosphere and created great craters all around the world. However, the majority of the material was blown out into space. Drawn in by their gravity, a large portion crashed into the moon and nearby planets. Even today, much of this space ice is still flying around, some in large chunks, which we refer to as ice comets." Rubbing his chin thoughtfully, Mr. Brooks asks Brian, "Is there any evidence to collaborate these events?"

"Sure!" Brian confidently spoke as he continued, "How else would you explain the many giant meteor craters with no meteorites in them, either on earth or on the moon? In addition, how do you explain the thousands of warm climate animals found frozen solid at both the North and South Poles? Especially the mammoths, some found standing up with food still in their mouths! In order for this to have occurred, they would have had to be flash-frozen in minutes by an ice dump of at least minus three hundred degrees Fahrenheit.

Besides, how else would you explain that organic matter must be buried quickly and deeply to fossilize according to physics laws? Because animals and plants that die on or near the surface are soon consumed by other organisms. The Devastation is the only plausible explanation for the existence of a worldwide fossil record.

What's more, it is well documented that the Earth's atmosphere is reducing, harmful rays from the sun are increasing, and the tectonic plates are still shifting. This shifting is now causing the most earthquakes recorded in modern history, and volcanic eruptions are at an all-time high!"

Mr. Brooks stood up and started pacing back and forth the entire length of the room, shooting out questions, "If this has been going on for millions of years, why aren't we all dead by now? In addition, how much longer can this go on before it does kill us all? And, why do you think our scientists have gotten it so wrong?"

Brian, entertained by Mr. Brook's demeanor, said, "That's three questions!" Then he responded, "NUMBER-1...It hasn't been going on for millions of years! NUMBER-2...Not much longer! NUMBER-3...Government grants!" Mr. Brooks' jaw dropped when he heard the answers.

Suddenly everything stopped, as a series of three taps each came from the control room window, made by one of the unseen onlookers. Immediately Mr. Brooks said, "Please excuse me; I will be right back." Then he quickly exited the room.

No one spoke, so Brian sat back in his chair and took a sip of his water, and waited. He could hear multiple, muffled voices excitedly babbling about something from behind the glass, but he could not make out what they were saying. Soon the babbling stopped. A few seconds later, Mr. Brooks re-entered the room. He asked all of the other agents to please leave, then he sat down directly across from Brian.

"Brian," Mr. Brooks said in a very somber voice, "We have a couple of our finest scientists who have put together a list of questions they want me to ask you." Brian just said, "No." "No!" Mr. Brooks exclaimed.

Brian followed up by saying, "Everyone agreed to the terms of this interview. If they want to ask me their questions, all they have to do is come in here and ask me. Face to face! If not, I go on with my story and ignore their questions." Brian just sat there waiting for Mr. Brooks to respond.

When he did respond, he was extremely stern. "Brian, you are not in charge here! You will have to remain here until we get what we want!"

Brian smiled and said, "What you said you wanted was to know what I know. Is that still the objective of this session, or is the objective to make me conform to your point of view? If it's to make me conform, we will both have failed in meeting our objectives." At that point, Brian stopped talking.

Mr. Brooks stared intently at Brian for a moment, then abruptly stood up and left the room. Once again, Brian could hear the muffled voices in the other room. However, this time they were getting much louder! Over two hours went by as Brian sits motionless in his chair with his eyes closed.

Meanwhile, in the other room, Mr. Brooks, Agent Cartwright, and the other agents, along with the two Scientists, Dr. Shook and Dr. Gibson, try to hash out the situation.

"Okay, doctors." Mr. Brooks said, "Mr. Gregory is refusing to answer your questions unless you ask him yourselves. Therefore, I suggest we all go back in there and put this thing to rest." Dr. Gibson said excitedly, "We are not going to give him the satisfaction of making us do what he wants!"

Mr. Brooks reminded them, "It's what we agreed to. There is no danger and no reason not to!" The doctors still refused, claiming it would be compromising their authority. After more than an hour of these one-sided negotiations, the doctors just said, "*We're not going in there*!"

Frustrated by their hesitation, Agent Cartwright gets angry and starts to rebuke the two scientists, "What's your problem? This guy is as harmless as a butterfly! Why do you *not* want to ask him the questions that *you* wanted him to answer?"

Mr. Brooks jumps in, "You two have wasted almost two hours making excuse after excuse of why you cannot ask your own questions to this man. Tell me now! Is there *anything* he has told us that can be *proven* to be untrue?"

The good doctors looked at each other, and Dr. Shook answered slowly and carefully, "Well...No...But what he is claiming has never been documented, proven, or published in any reputable science journal, anywhere!"

Mr. Brooks couldn't believe what he was hearing! With fire in his eyes, he declared, "If you don't go in there immediately, I will have Agent Jones escort your worthless butts back to your laboratories." "*You can't do that*!" Shrilled Dr. Gibson. "It's done!" Declared Mr. Brooks. "Agent Jones...Get them out of here!" Both scientists, huffing and puffing, were led away.

Agent Cartwright turns to Mr. Brooks and says, "What's going on here? Have you ever been in an interview where the guy answers the questions before you ask them? And all the doctor's questions have done is slow down the process of finding out what Mr. Gregory knows! I think we need to go back in there, apologize, shut up, and let him talk!" Mr. Brooks just nodded his head and said, "I'm getting too old for this crap. Let's go."

Brian quickly opened his eyes when he heard the turn of the doorknob. Mr. Brooks entered first and glanced at Brian with an apologetic grin. Agent Cartwright follows with a clipboard in his hand and the same embarrassed look on his face. Brian stands up, and all three men face each other.

Mr. Brooks stated, "Brian, I apologize for the way I spoke earlier...No excuse for that. I hope we can continue with your story." "Yeah, Brian, me too." Agent Cartwright quietly injected. "All's forgiven." Brian said, "But we've got a lot of ground to cover."

GOING TO NOA

Brian begins again, "As we discussed earlier, the Devastation wrecked the Earth's surface, as well as the atmosphere. Almost everything was destroyed! The few survivors set out to repopulate the earth. Most of the smaller wild animals did well on their own. However, many of the larger and domesticated kinds had to be bred in corrals, which surrounded the stacked stone dwellings that the Noaans built to temporarily house themselves. Even though their efforts were successful, the toll that the devastation had taken on the environment was becoming evident in man, plant, and animal within a few years.

Although man's intellect had remained intact, their bodies started to suffer from fatigue and new illnesses. Plants lost much of their ability to adapt to extreme conditions, and the animals became aggressive towards each other and man in their struggle to survive.

Furthermore, by the end of the first century, the ever-growing population had spread out and started rebuilding their once great civilizations. At first, this seemed to be a good thing, but it quickly led to a previously unforeseen problem, the loss of ancient knowledge! This loss of knowledge came about as the young moved away, and the elders, who had previously overseen the training of the young, were left behind to help build up the more established civilizations.

At the same time, the world was being divided by family groups vying for domination. Primarily due to a breakdown in communications caused by an abrupt change in languages. The division became even worse as the rising waters from the melting glaciers isolated the continents and the people on them. Many of the new coastal cities had to be abandoned as their populations were forced to move to higher ground.

By the time humanity had spread to the farthest continents, many of the young pioneers had lost most, if not all, the knowledge of their heritage. Resulting in many of them being reduced to primitive lifestyles and Truth being replaced by superstition.

In a search for a solution, the elders came together to preserve their way of life. Hence, with an acute knowledge of physics and engineering, they devised a plan to build manmade environments to mimic the original. The downside of the project was the only way to build these civilizations would be to go underground.

Many of their engineers had already surveyed the emptied water chambers lifted up by the massive rolling of the earth's crust during the devastation. The chambers were enormous and covered large portions of the continents beneath the higher mountainous regions. They were miles deep in places, with few access points, which would make them easier to keep hidden from the quickly growing population on the surface.

Furthermore, the Noaans would have to limit themselves primarily to the chambers for their plan to work except for maintenance and surveillance. Needless to say, not everyone was excited about the plan!

Therefore, those who wished to go went in! A large majority, however, chose to remain on the surface, and they did so. The ones who decided to stay on the surface are the ancestors of all known people groups today. Despite our differences, we are all one people.

Over the years, however, some of the disgruntled Noaans chose to return to the surface. For most of them, ambition was the driving factor. These were the ones who wished to rule over the diminished surface population, and they became great warrior kings, such as Og and Anak. They actually convinced themselves and others that they were gods, including Apollo, Zeus, Hermes, and Thor. I can only guess this is one of the reasons for the government's determined interest in the Noaans.

Nevertheless, one hundred and sixty-five years after the devastation, the Noaans were well into building an elaborate civilization in their new subterranean home. The first order of business was to secure the chamber's environment. To accomplish this, all access points to the surface had to be sealed. This was for the colony's security and allowed the air pressure to build up to optimum levels.

In the meantime, the agriculturalist had to develop a way to transfer the light of the sun from the surface to the caverns. They did this so they could cultivate the appropriate plants to produce adequate oxygen levels. Non-solar energy was also produced by the use of hydroelectric generation systems. The water still draining from some of the higher chambers was used to power these systems.

Next, the architects designed and built numerous cities, towns, and farming communities with the ability to expand with the population. The architecture was in a beautiful ancient design, but with incredible technology. The technology is so advanced that it included many solar-powered innovations that we do not have even today.

They also built fabulous gardens and game reserves to house the animals that would be endangered on the surface. They had designed these reserves for the animals, some because of their size, which needed higher oxygen concentrations to survive.

Finally, the surveyors prospected many other caverns around the world to maximize the potential for growth. Noa was the sixth of the eleven Noaan civilizations. Joktan was the first of the civilizations built, and Jerah was the last.

Noa is not a city. It is more the size of Italy in square miles. Where exactly is it? Well, I don't know, but it is somewhere under the Appalachians, and it's deep. Deep enough to increase the air pressure by an average of eight pounds per square inch to almost twenty-three pounds per square inch. The oxygen levels were also raised and maintained at a level of about thirty percent.

The temperature hovers around sixty-five degrees, with very low humidity. It felt chilly to me, but Sada explained that it was perfect for their size and metabolism. However, the Noaans were kind enough to provide me with clothing specifically made for me. All these things are a part of the history which I was taught in Noa."

Agent Cartwright sheepishly raised his hand. Kinda chuckling, Brian told him, "Dave, you don't have to raise your hand." Dave said, "Okay. Sorry. But, I have a question about Sada. You said he was small for his age at 8'-11". How old is he?" Brian grinned and told him, "Sada is eighty-seven years old! Noaans typically obtain their full height by the age of one-hundred and ten, so he should have been about ten feet tall by his age. Furthermore, the average lifespan of a Noaan is about three hundred and seventy years."

Brian paused for a moment and asked, "Mr. Brooks...Would you mind if I call you Mel? I understand that you may not want to be called "Mel Brooks," so if it's a problem, I can continue to call you Mr. Brooks." Mr. Brooks smiled and replied, "No. Mel will be fine."

Brian stood up and stretched and said, "I've been talking for a while...Do you have any questions so far?" "Are you kidding?" exclaimed Mel. Brian said jokingly, "Shoot...Now that's just an expression!" Everybody in the room laughed. You could even hear a few chuckles from the control room. As a result, the tension was gone!

THE NOAANS

Mel said, "I do have a few questions, and I will give them to you one at a time. First, what can you tell us about Sada and the other Noaans…families, friends, personalities, etc.…?"
"I was hoping you'd ask this question," Brian said excitedly.

"Sada, now he's a special guy. He was my trainer, along with one of the elders named Yerimi. Sada treated me like a little brother, and the other Noaans treated me like one of their children. I did not mind, though, because I quickly learned that a sixty-year-old man, who has only the use of nine percent of his brain, is a child, compared to a ten-year-old with the use of eighty percent of theirs

Once, I made the mistake of challenging a nine-year-old to a game of chess…I lost…Badly! Chess is considered by the Noaans to be a child's game, much like Tic-Tac-Toe is to us, and for the same reasons."

Yerimi, on the other hand, was all business! He is two hundred and eighty-seven years old and has been training people like me for over a hundred years. Yerimi was 12'-2" tall and weighed about eight hundred pounds! When he stood up, his belt was above my head. He has been an elder for thirty-six years.

All Noaans become elders at two hundred and fifty-one years old. The elder's responsibilities are to help train the youth, manage the current civilizations, and plan for expansion. For the past five hundred years, they have been accelerating the expansion of the population in preparation for the seventh millennium.

Furthermore, The Noaans are a beautiful people and are very well proportioned, due to their healthy lifestyle. It was commonplace to see one of them sprinting across the countryside for long periods, at over thirty miles an hour. They are very powerful and have extremely quick reflexes. As for their appearance, Noaans dress very modestly, in diverse types of clothing, which reflects their individual taste.

However, the first thing I noticed about them was that they had a joy, which too often seemed to be missing in our culture. From my observations, I think the source of the Noaans' peace stemmed from their understanding of their origins and individual purpose in life. They seemed to know what their gifts were and how best to use them.

Still, the thing I enjoyed most of all was spending time with Sada. He was my protector and friend. He often told me stories about his father, Rada-

BarSet. Rada was a pilot, and his job was to fly surveillance missions on the surface, usually at night. However, one night Rada and Raab, Sada's older brother, died in an airship accident near Roswell, New Mexico, in 1947. Sada was only seventeen years old at the time, but he loved his father very much. It honored me greatly when he told me that I had his father's sense of humor. Sada and Yerimi also taught me the customs and traditions of the Noaans and pre-devastation history. They took me on tours to Noa's power facilities, farms, gardens, parks, and the most incredible animal reserves.

The reserves have every animal you can imagine and some you would not believe. They actually had forty-seven kinds of dragons." "Dragons?" Dave exclaimed, "They really have dragons?" Brian said, "Yes, they do!" Mel, looking confused and holding up his hands, said, "Okay. You just lost me! I'm supposed to report to my superiors that you actually saw forty-seven dragons?"

"Noooo." Brian answered, "I said forty-seven kinds of dragons. There were over three hundred in total." "Oh crap!" Mel complained, "I really am getting too old for this!" Brian, with a silly look on his face, says, "With everything I've told you today, *this* is what you have trouble believing?"

Brian jokingly says, "Haven't you ever heard of the Chinese dragon wars, the knights in shining armor killing the dragons? Heck, even the prophet Daniel in one of the non-biblical historical accounts, killed a dragon with a vat full of grease and hair! Yet you still don't believe in dragons. Tsk, tsk, tsk." "No, I Don't!" Mel said forcibly.

Nevertheless, Brian persisted, "How about all the triceratops, velociraptors, brachiosaurus, and the other dragon fossils that have been found?" "They weren't dragons! They were dinosaurs!" Mel proclaimed loudly.

Brian explained, "I'm sorry to break it to you, Mel, but they were all called dragons up until 1841." Then, while making quotation marks with his fingers, Brian said. "That's when some 'scientists' decided to start calling them dinosaurs! But the way I see it, since your so-called 'scientists' don't have any dinosaurs, and the Noaans do. I guess they can call them dragons if they want to!"

Looking distraught, Dave said, "But, Brian...I have been taught my whole life that dinosaurs died out millions of years ago." "I know Dave. I know." Brian said supportively. Dave just stood there for a while with a blank look on his face. Mel was looking a little rattled himself, leaning forward, looking down at the floor, and shaking his head. Brian asked them, "Do you have any more questions about dragons?" "Hell No!" Mel blurted out.

Brian continued, "Although Sada is not a prophet, by anyone's definition, he is a master scholar and philosopher! He explained to me that to *muse* means to think, and to *amuse* means not to think.

This is why it concerns him that we have turned to amusing ourselves as a form of entertainment. The Noaans see our children wasting their lives playing violent video games and the adults watching hours of television every day! Furthermore, he told me that taking time to muse on something truly important is more productive, rewarding, and fulfilling than looking for ways to escape reality.

He also told me that a great example of how we misunderstand intelligence is the TV show 'Big Bang Theory. Have any of you seen it?" They all acknowledged, "Yeah…Sure." So Brian asked, "Who on the show is supposed to be the most intelligent?" Dave answered. "Sheldon!" and everyone agreed. Then he asked, "Who would you say is the most dysfunctional?" Again, they all agreed on Sheldon. So Brian asked, "Can you explain how that is even possible?" Everyone looked around at everyone else, but no one had an answer!

Brian answered his own question with, "According to Yerimi, Intelligence is the individual's ability to retain knowledge. Knowledge is the information we choose to put into our minds. Wisdom is the ability to discern if knowledge is true, so it can be used productively. Therefore, above all, we should seek wisdom!

Yerimi also told me that you can usually spot a wise person by their humility because someone wise realizes how little they actually know. On the other hand, the foolish are those who love to proclaim themselves to be wise!" The reason I'm sharing this with you now is so you will understand what I have to tell you next."

When Brian said this, everyone in the room, everyone in the control room, and everyone monitoring this interview had only one thing on their minds! What is Brian going to tell them next?

WHAT THEY KNOW

Then, Brian continued. "As you have obviously noticed, I have had access to a great deal of information pertaining to today's events. Including names and locations, all linked to what has taken place. Furthermore, each event has occurred in the exact order I was told they would.

For example, I knew where to go. I knew I had to call Renae and that you would be listening for my call. I knew how long it would take your team to arrive at the general store. I knew who was on duty and in which SUV you would put me. I knew the names of each agent in the vehicle and who would be in charge of the detail.

Furthermore, I knew who would remain in the room when we arrived and who would be listening from the control booth, i.e., Dr. Shook and Dr. Gibson, along with Seth and Larry, the A/V techs.

I know what your objectives are and what the secret goals are of those who are listening in. Even of those who are unknown to you! Finally, I know full well the consequences of telling the rest of my story. I know all this because my friends

Sada and Yerimi told me in detail how today's events would unfold.

Therefore, you must realize that the technology of the Noaans is beyond our understanding! They monitor every public and private record, phone call, email, website, and communications, whether it be government, private or military.

They know which senate bill will pass, which stock is going to tank, and where the terrorists will strike next. They also know what each government is planning to do and who is pulling their strings. They know what is happening on the surface better than the people on the surface do!

What's more, they hear every word and see everything going on in this room at this very moment. They can see you, those in the control room, as well as everyone else watching this interview."

Brian points out, "Sada, as well as all of the other Noaans, study their enemy and his tactics. They have studied every false religion throughout time, from Baal to Jim Jones. They have memorized every text and passage of every religion that has been on this planet since day one. And there really was a Day One!

They have warriors who fight and die, just as we do. However, they do not fight for power or riches. They fight for us because we are their commission!

What's more, Noaans are just people! They are not psychics, magicians, angels, or gods. The Noaans are just like us. Yet, they understand the true powers at war in the universe and especially in this world. They know the truth because they know the Truth!"

As Brian was saying all of this, Mel and Dave were sitting in their chairs spellbound. Suddenly Mel stood up and started walking around in small half-circles muttering something to himself. For a second, he stopped in place, turned to Brian, and asked, "What is Truth?"

Brian leaned forward in his chair with his elbows resting on his knees and answered, "Truth knows where you came from, where you are now and where you are going. Most of all, Truth is knowing why! With both hands holding his head, Mel asks, "Where do you find the truth? Where do you start?"

Brian sits up straight in his chair, smiles, and starts again, "We have been promised by the One who created everything that if we seek for the Truth, we will find it!" Mel very pointedly says,

"If it's so easy, why doesn't everyone find the truth?"

Brian explained, "Truth isn't easy! Truth can be scary! Truth can be humbling! Truth may even require personal sacrifice! Nevertheless, sometime in your life, even if you have not searched out Truth, Truth will come to you. Everyone past, present, and future has, or will face Truth! The wise will receive the Truth...The foolish will not. The Word explains it like this, Because of their lust, they are willfully ignorant! Wisdom is accepting Truth by faith!

More agitated than ever, Mel asks, "Okay...What is faith? What is the Word? And how do you get the wisdom to recognize truth when you see it?"

Brian leans forward again and says, "Faith...Faith is the substance of things hoped for, the evidence of things not seen. The Word...In the beginning was the Word, the Word was with God and the Word was God. And Wisdom...If any of you lack wisdom, let him ask of God, that giveth to all men liberally and upbraideth not and it shall be given him."

There were no more questions. Everyone sat staring off into space as they tried to grasp the meaning of all this. Brian, seeing that he had their full attention, started again.

THE WORLD CHANGED

Now looking very serious, Brian says to his audience, "Now, I will tell you about the Devastation. What was changed and how it unfolded.

The 'Devastation' is better known today as the 'Flood of Noah.' As you have more than likely figured out, the Noaans are the descendants of Noah, Shem, Ham, and Japheth, who are also the ancestors of all mankind today.

Noah was a man, who walked in the way of the Creator, and by faith, according to the Creator's design, he built the ark. Although everyone was called, only eight actually chose to enter. There was also every kind of beast of the earth with breath in their nostrils. Then came the devastation!

The Noaans call it the Devastation because it is the most accurate way to describe it. The Flood was just the most obvious result of the devastation. However, many other events took place, unseen to humanity at the time. This is the account of the events, which caused the flood.

First, Noah and his family entered the ark, and God himself sealed up the door. For seven days, they prayed, worshiped, and waited.

After seven days, all around the planet, the crust of the earth ripped open. The chambers of compressed water, which were many miles below the surface, exploded upward with unimaginable force. This compacted water release carried with it enormous rocks and debris, which shot up through the atmosphere and ruptured the protective barrier above.

Because of the drastic pressure differences between the earth's atmosphere and the vacuum of space, the ice barrier fractured and was blown outward into space. All this took place within the first few hours of the devastation

As a result of this and the following seismic events, the atmospheric pressure and oxygen levels decreased drastically, and most surface areas became oceans. Finally, the once consistent global temperatures started fluctuating greatly because the new tilt of the planet caused the earth to have its first seasons.

The flood came as the waters being blown out of the crust were dispersed throughout the atmosphere. Once the atmosphere was saturated, the water fell as torrential rains, slowly dissipating over forty days.

Furthermore, the earth's crust started sinking down due to the emptying water chambers collapsing underneath and the weight of the massive ice dump from space. This resulted in the water covering the entire face of the earth within a few weeks.

By the fifth month, the effects of the water release and the ice dump were so significant that they tilted the earth off its zero axis. This occurred when the crust shifted because of the rapid movement of the water underneath and the crust's weight above.

The shift was so severe that the tectonic plates of the entire planet started moving at an incredible rate. As they moved, they crashed together with enough force to push up entire mountain ranges.

The world before had mountains with a maximum elevation of approximately five thousand feet. However, the crashing together and massive movement of the plates raised some seafloors by many thousands of feet into some of the highest of today's mountain ranges. This is why fossilized clams can be found on the peak of Mount Everest.

Furthermore, as the larger chambers collapsed in on themselves, enormous portions of the surface sank down for miles in places. This caused the water to rush in from the higher ground, and the massive tidal waves started dissipating.

The new surface of the earth was decimated. Death and destruction were everywhere. The waters churning the ground beneath buried the majority of the plants and animals. The organic materials buried deep were compressed into coal and petroleum. Those buried shallow became the fossil record. Continent size glaciers created by the massive ice dump covered much of the northern and southernmost parts of the globe. Nowhere on the planet had escaped the Devastation.

Furthermore, over the next few hundred years, the glaciers melted back. The dry ground, before the flood, had covered about eighty percent of the planet, was reduced to approximately twenty-five percent.

The flood also produced giant lakes, when the valleys between mountain ranges trapped the water, preventing runoff. Many of these lakes disappeared once the following runoff caused them to breach their banks and drain. The most dramatic example of these overflows is in North America, where a breached dam, in just days, washed out what we now call The Grand Canyon.

The waters from the flood had been upon the earth for about five months when God caused them to assuage. Soon after, He revealed to Noah that the waters were receding. In the seventh month, God brought the ark to rest in Ararat, a mountainous region in eastern Turkey.

By the tenth month, the surrounding mountain peaks were visible. Then, God caused a great wind to blow across the surface, to dry out the land. Finally, one year, one month, and ten days after Noah and his family entered the ark, they took their first steps into the new world. This was the Devastation! The judgment by water."

HISTORY

Brian looks around at Dave and Mel, who looked a little dazed, and asked, "How you holding up?" "We're good," Mel answered. So, Brian continued, "Now I will tell you about the survivors and their work to preserve the ancient knowledge entrusted to them.

The Noaans have a copy of every document ever published. However, what they value most are the Yahshua Scripts. These scripts include every scroll and tablet of scripture dating back to the beginning. They are a detailed documentation of the history of man. Therefore, from creation until the present, there remains an eyewitness account of everything God has done.

The Yahshua Scripts were handed down from generation to generation throughout pre-devastation history, from Adam to Noah. Each generation safeguarded them and added their part, as led by the Spirit of God to do so. Soon after the Devastation, Noah passed the documents down to Shem, who added his part along with his brothers, Ham and Japheth. Others, chosen by God, added their genealogies, history, and His prophecies later. This was not for their benefit, however. It was for ours.

To preserve these documents, copies were distributed to the Noaans and those who chose to remain on the surface. In this way, the Noaans would have them, even though they would be in the isolation of their underground refuge.

Meanwhile, just as their fathers had done, the elders passed down the information through oral dissertation. This was the primary way of sharing the information up until the time that Israel went into Egypt. The youth at this time were still disciplined enough and had the intellectual ability to memorize and communicate vast amounts of information.

This is why the written Word as we know it was not as essential in order for them to pass along the information. This could also be one way of verifying His written word as He referred to Himself as the God of Abraham, Isaac, and Jacob.

On the other hand, following the people of Israel's time in Egypt, their knowledge, learning abilities, and lifespans had all diminished, mostly due to the environment and their lack of training. Foreknowing this, God had prepared a way to pass the documents down to His people in a form that could be easily understood and dispersed worldwide.

To begin this process, God chose Moses to be His first messenger. Therefore, during his exile to Midian from Egypt, God called Moses to record the story of His servant, Job, through the guidance of the Holy Spirit. Soon after, Moses was led to compile the historic scripts, written and passed down from Adam to Jacob, into the Book of Genesis.

Through the years, God's servants have recorded their history and His plan for humanity. This was to help us prepare for His visitation and soon-coming Kingdom. As a result, the documents of the Bible were delivered to man and Noaans alike. Therefore, just as He had promised, God preserved His word throughout all generations.

Meanwhile, those who wished to deceive humanity for their own benefit produced many counterfeits and forgeries. This is the true motive and method behind the work of the enemy! Nevertheless, even though these corrupted documents have deceived many, the Truth has always triumphed because God said it would.

For example, in the first century, as the New Testament was being written, Paul warned us about those who were paraphrasing the writings in a way that would change the true meaning of the message. However, the true message endured. This is why the Bible is completely true and scientifically accurate in every way.

With man, talk is cheap. However, when God speaks, the worlds come into existence, life springs up from nothing, blind men see, lame men walk, and dead men are raised to life. Even the very definition of the word Universe means (Uni.) Single, (Verse) Spoken Word. God said, "Let There Be" And there was.

Furthermore, it only makes sense that the Creator of the whole universe would provide His creation with His Word. Therefore, He provided them with an owner's manual to tell them how to live the best life they can and someone to fix them when they are broken! And He did.

Before I conclude my story, I want to go on record and thank Special Agent Dave Cartwright and Mr. Mel Brooks for their kindness, honesty, and attention. I also want to go or record to say, when I finish sharing my story with these gentlemen, I will never share it again."

Mel interrupts, "What do you mean that you will never share your story again?" Dave just sat there, curiously awaiting the answer. Brian calmly said, "It is my choice. It is, the way it is." Mel stood up, turned around a couple of times as if he didn't know which way he wanted to go!

While he was doing this, Dave and Brian watched and waited to hear what he was thinking. He finally turned towards Brian and said, "Brian, earlier today, Dave asked me to tell him what was going on here." Mel turned and looked directly at Dave and said, "Agent Cartwright, I have no idea!"

While walking around the room, flapping his arms in the air, Mel ranted, "This has been the most confusing interview that I've ever conducted, and I've been doing this for over twenty-five years!" He turned back to face Brian and pointed out, "I understand what you are saying and why you have so many people worried. The things you have told us go against the belief system of some *very* powerful people! Some of whom will do almost anything to stop you from telling anyone else! The Noaans must have warned you about this!"

"They did," Brian answered. "But do you think I could've kept all this to myself?" Now, as Mel was pondering the question, Dave suddenly spoke up! "What on earth were the Noaans thinking putting you in this situation? How can a people who claim to be so noble make you give up everything and endanger yourself like this? For a message? Even a message like this?"

Brian walked over to Dave and put his hand on his shoulder, and said, "They didn't make me. I could have returned to my family and my old way of life if I had agreed to never tell anyone what I know. Agreeing to do this was my decision. It was the final test of my training. To Choose. So, I did! It was my choice and my choice alone. I chose to serve something bigger than myself, something bigger than anything! Besides, I want everyone to know the Truth!"

"But, you said that you would never tell this story again," Mel mumbled aloud to himself. Brian leaned over and quietly told him. "Yes, Mel, I did! What's more, there is something you should know before I continue. The final part of this message may be dangerous for you to hear as well. Therefore I will only tell you, as much as you are willing to hear!"

THE MOVEMENT

Brian went straight to it. "This part of the message from the Noaans is about the worldwide political Movement to globalize the planet's governments. Although this Movement has been going on for hundreds of years, it has gained a tremendous amount of traction in the past twenty years. Furthermore, the Movement has almost succeeded in three of its primary goals.

The First Goal is to strategically destabilize the governments of countries that believe in national sovereignty. National sovereignty opposes the Movement's efforts to transfer the governing authority of a country away from the elected leadership and to a central committee or governing body assigned by them.

They started the process by victimizing minority people groups while at the same time pretending to represent their interests. This dual role was effective in exciting the groups to first protest and then rise up against their elected leadership.

The eventual result would strip the people of their right to govern themselves and reduce them from individuals into victim groups who depend on the government to provide for their every need. By replacing opportunity with dependence, the government will decide themselves what the people need!

The Movement will also plan and execute terrorist attacks, which they use to establish fear and prejudice in the population. This fear and prejudice will produce a house divided against itself by race and religion. Resulting in making the government appear as the only source of security.

Finally, they will infiltrate and monopolize the media, both conservative and liberal alike. Once achieved, the Movement will get both sides to divide the people by pitting them against one another. Thus breaking down all forms of meaningful communications. The results of this will foster distrust in the media and devalue freedom of speech. When the freedom of speech is gone, the Movement can dictate the information published by the state-controlled media.

When they achieve the *First Goal*, the people will give their governments controlled by the Movement's own special interest groups the license to ignore due process and overstep their authority.

Their Second Goal is to secularize society by radicalizing groups that worship their religion! Thus painting God as false. And through the teaching of erroneous science as fact, the Movement will deceive the world's youth into believing that there is no truth. Therefore, when the *Second Goal* is achieved, the world's future leaders will trust government instead of God! The government will become their god.

The Third Goal is to control the now cynical, atheistic, oppressed, and fearful peoples of the world. Those who have been preconditioned to look to their governments to solve all of their problems. The next logical step will be to bring the world's governments into a cooperative, which would quickly evolve into a One World Government.

When the Movement achieves all three Goals, *in the name of peace*, the new One World Government will establish laws to regulate all freedoms, including ownership rights, freedom of the press, and religion. The people of faith will suffer the worst persecution imaginable because the rest of the world will consider them dissidents.

The Noaans, as well as the other Bible-believing peoples, have intensively studied the scriptures. They know that the prophecies of the Bible, pertaining to the rise and fall of the empires and kingdoms of the past, have always come true in every detail. They also know from prophecy and the proof of history that the prophecies about the future will also come true. Therefore, the Movement will do everything they can to stop them and squelch the Message. Because the one thing which is most detrimental to the Movement is Truth!

What's more, the scriptures have factually detailed the creation, the genealogies, the Devastation, and most precisely, the first coming, life, death, and resurrection of Jesus Christ...Yahshua. Moreover, the scholars have seen that the beginning of the seventh millennium is near.

Yet many people have ignored the extraordinary evidence of the Bible truths by their own choice. Some of the proof includes Noah's ark, found in the mountains of Ararat, the chariot wheels, and human and horse remains found on the bottom of the Red Sea. The ashen remains of Sodom and the other cities of the plain, which have been found along the Dead Sea's west side. And the true Mount Sinai with the ancient encampment in Midian found in western Saudi Arabia. Even though all these are visible on google earth.

Most of all, the crucifixion site of Christ, with the cutouts where the Romans displayed the criminal's offenses, found between the Garden Tomb and Golgotha. The massive stone missing for almost two thousand years was found lying on the ground directly in front of the center cross whole, along with the remnants of a first-century church's walls built around the site.

Subsequently, God has revealed the evidence of our faith and of His past judgments to the world. Nevertheless, as in Noah and Sodom's times, the world has denied that these events have taken place. Most people still refuse to accept that there is to be a second coming and final judgment. Yahshua said like this, "If they hear not Moses and the prophets, neither will they be persuaded though one rose from the dead."

However, before there was a Movement, before the Devastation, before Adam, before Lucifer and the angels, before there was light, before there was a world, even before there was time, there was the Word. Not one of these events had taken place that God had not foreseen.

He wanted perfect people to share all things with, and to love. God knew what He wanted and what He had to do to accomplish it. He created a perfect universe and gave His creation, Choice! He did this knowing that most of His creation would not choose Him. Nevertheless, He created them. He then took on the form of His creation to live, suffer and die so those who would choose Him could be with Him forever.

Over the years, priests, teachers, and preachers have told us that we all shall stand before God. We shall not! I will stand before God by myself, and you will stand before God by yourself. God will accept those who wear the robe of Christ's righteousness. On the other hand, those who appear in the filthy rags of their own righteousness, He will not! Therefore, Grace is the only thing that can save us! The Grace of God, through Yahshua. This is the choice that all people of accountable age and even the angels have had to make."

Brian, with a peaceful expression, said, "This completes my story. My part of the Message is done!"

"Thank goodness!" Dave said, sounding exhausted. Mel nervously talked up and asked, "Brian, what do you expect us to do with your message?" Brian's answer, however, took Dave and Mel off guard, "It is not my message!" In almost perfect unison, Mel and Dave anxiously Asked. "Then whose message is it?" "It's yours!" Brian said. Mel, sounding aggravated, shouted! "What are we supposed to do with it?" Brian just said, "Choose."

Mel was feeling extremely nervous and went over to the bar to get himself another bottle of water. As he was guzzling it down, he froze, staring at the mirrored window. He was so absorbed in Brian's story, the reality of how many people were watching and listening just now sank in. Dave was still sitting in his chair watching Brian, waiting for him to say something. Anything!

Brian said very seriously, "That's really all I had to say! So...Mel, have I told you as much as you are willing to hear?" Mel's eyebrow raised in surprise, and he replied, "Yes, Brian...Thank you." Brian then acknowledged, "Mel, it's time to say it!"

At that point, sitting up straight and looking even more confused than ever, Dave turned to Mel and asked, "Say what?" Mel just stood there in silence, staring at the glass. Brian says, "It has to be said, Mel...Do you want me to tell them?" Mel looked down at the floor for a minute and said, "No. I will say it."

"SAY WHAT?" Dave demanded. "It's time to go!" Mel declared. All three men slowly moved to the middle of the room, and Brian said, "Thanks, guys." He shook their hands and sat down to wait. There was silence for about three minutes, then they heard footsteps in the hallway.

ROOM 2028

Four armed guards abruptly came in the door and immediately surrounded Brian. Dave and Mel stepped back out of the way. Two other men came in that Mel and Dave did not recognize. The one who was obviously in charge said to Brian, "Mr. Gregory, you have been deemed a clear and present danger to the national security of the United States!" The mysterious man nodded to the guards, who rapidly handcuffed Brian and marched him out of the room. The two unknown men turned to Mel and Dave and told them, "You may not talk to anyone about anything you've heard today! You will be debriefed in the morning. Go home!" Then, they turned around and left as quickly as they came in.

Mel and Dave stood there in shock and disbelief. Dave asked, "What the. Who were those guys? And by what authority did they take Brian to...wherever they are taking him?" "I'm sure I don't know." Mel said, "Let's get out of here." As they were walking out through the steel corridor, Mel whispered, "We need to talk! I have some things I need to check out first. Meet me at the Waffle House at eight-thirty." They went to the parking lot and drove off in different directions as if they were going home.

In the meantime, Brian was taken farther down the main hallway to a room with an assortment of medical equipment, including a magnetic resonance scanner. The guards ordered him to strip. Then they conducted an exhaustive body search and made him stand naked in a small square painted on the floor.

A few minutes later, the two scientists entered the room. They checked his heart rate, lung function and took several blood samples. They put Brian through the scanner for a head-to-toe search to make sure he had no implants. Brian submitted himself to hours of humiliating procedures. Upon completing their examination, they threw him some bright yellow coveralls and a pair of slippers. Not a word was spoken during the entire process.

Following the examination, Brian was moved even farther down the hall to room 2028. There the guards roughly sat him down in a steel-framed chair, handcuffed him to a steel table, and left the room. Unlike room 2021, this room was stark, with harsh lighting and gray concrete walls. There were no mirrors or cameras that Brian could see. However, this is exactly where Brian was told he would be.

About eight twenty-five, Mel arrived at the Waffle House to see Dave already sitting at a table. He went in and joined him. As soon as he sat down, the waitress asked, "Ya want some coffee?" "Two coffees, black. Thanks!" Mel replied. She poured them a cup, then Dave asked Mel, "Who were those guys, and why are we being treated as outsiders?" Mel responded, "I was thinking the same thing on the way over here. They must be with Homeland. I think that they think we know too much." Dave, still stirring his coffee, said, "Yeah...me too...What do we do now?"

Mel answered, "I have spent the past few hours researching the things Brian told us. To keep it under the radar, I went down to an internet café in Knoxville and started googling. Once I got started, I couldn't seem to stop! The amount of information available is incredible! Not once in my life have I ever questioned the things I've been taught.

Brian was definitely right about one thing. We are taught what to think, not how to think! What's more, I went on Google Earth and saw the remains of Noah's Ark, the Red Sea crossing site, and the burnt remains of Sodom and Gomorrah, just like Brian said. It's absolutely insane how we have allowed ourselves to be led around like sheep!"

When Mel finished, Dave said, "I did a little research on my own but in another direction.

You would not believe how much of what is taught as scientific proof has been proven wrong! Nevertheless, no one will speak out about it. The worst part is, it's all still in the textbooks!" Dave and Mel sat there for a couple more hours, drinking coffee and sharing their findings. At last, Dave said, "It's getting late! I guess we should head on home; our wives will be worried. So. What we gonna do now?"

Mel told him plainly, "We do what we were told to. We go home, think about it, and make a choice! Brian said this choice is ours to make for ourselves. I cannot decide for you, and you cannot decide for me. I almost wish I didn't know, but I do!" They stood up; Mel dropped a twenty on the table and told the waitress to keep the change. Finally, the two men shook hands and headed home.

Meanwhile, back in room 2028, Brian heard the door tumbler unlocking as four men entered the room and sat down across the table from him. They set several stacks of paperwork on the table, and the one in charge asked, "Brian, do you know who we are?" "Yes." Brian said, "You two are Mr. Lynn and Mr. Paulson with the HSA, and these are my favorite scientist, doctors Shook and Gibson." Mr. Lynn and Mr. Paulson never flinched. Dr. Shook and Dr. Gibson, however, were obviously nervous and were literally squirming in their seats.

Mr. Lynn asked, "Tell me how you know our names?" Brian answered, "You were listening to my first interview earlier, so you already know the answer to that question." In an intimidating manner, Mr. Lynn stated, "I want to hear it for myself!" Brian said calmly. "Listen to the playback. I have already told you my story."

Infuriated by Brian's response. Mr. Lynn said. "Do you think you're ever going to get out of here without answering my questions?" Brian looked Mr. Lynn directly in the eyes and said, "No." Mr. Lynn was fuming as Brian continued. "I have already told you as much as you are willing to hear."

That was the straw that broke the camel's back! Mr. Lynn said unemotionally, "So, you are refusing to cooperate with this investigation. Therefore, I have no alternative but to have you transferred to a maximum-security facility for further processing. Do you have anything to say for yourself?" Brian responded, "I will only be going, where I knew I would be going, by my own choice. I would not change a thing! However, I want you gentlemen to know that you have a choice as long as you have life. My choice is made. The choice now is *yours*!"

Mr. Lynn sat there staring at Brian with a determined, as ever look on his face. However, he failed to notice that Mr. Paulson's expression had changed into one of thoughtful concern. When Mr. Lynn finally got up to leave, Brian glanced over at Mr. Paulson, who was still staring at him and Brian nodded. Mr. Paulson nodded in return as if to say he understood. He scooped up the paperwork and followed the other men out of the room. Once again, Brian was left alone in the room.

After leaving the room, Mr. Lynn and the three other gentlemen assembled in the hallway. It was almost midnight, and they were all looking weary, so Mr. Lynn told them, "Go home, but be here at nine for Agent Cartwright's and Mr. Brook's debriefing."

As they turned to go, Mr. Lynn said, "Mr. Paulson, wait up. You were silent all evening! What is your take on this Brian Gregory character?" Mr. Paulson answered, "The things Mr. Gregory said today have been disturbing, to say the least. Do you think there may be any truth to them?" "Does it matter?" Mr. Lynn quipped. Mr. Paulson responded, "I guess not. Good night." Then, he turned and leisurely headed up the steel corridor towards the parking lot.

THE GRAY ROOM

Mel and Dave found themselves sitting in the gray room the following morning, silently waiting for their supervisors to debrief them. However, they weren't too surprised when Mr. Lynn and Mr. Paulson entered the room instead of their supervisors. "Did you sleep well?" Mr. Lynn asked. "Not a wink!" Mel replied quickly. Dave added, "Me either." Mr. Lynn asked, "Why not?" Dave looked at the two HSA agents and asked sternly, "Why do you think?"

Mr. Lynn sat thoughtfully for a moment, tapping his fingers on the table. When he finally did speak, he said, "Before we get started, I want you to know that the information you witnessed yesterday has been deemed Classified. Therefore, discussing this information with anyone outside of this room would violate your oath and would be punishable by censure, termination, and/or imprisonment! Do you understand?" Mel and Dave both nodded in affirmation.

"Good!" said Mr. Lynn, and he continued, "Regarding the claims of Mr. Gregory, they have been proven to be false! However, they could still be a danger to the security of the United States and must be prevented from being made public. The US and other countries have been working on this problem for many years. They have spent millions of dollars investigating the disappearance of hundreds of people who had returned and made the same claims as Mr. Gregory. So. I just want to put this behind us! Therefore, I need you to sign a non-disclosure agreement before you leave today. Are there any questions?"

"A few," Mel said as he sat forward in his chair. "If his claims have been proven false, how could they be dangerous? The last time I looked, even wackos had the freedom of speech in this country! What's more, why would we be spending millions of dollars on a theory that has already been debunked? Why don't you bring Mr. Gregory in here and let your scientist ask their questions to him, face to face!"

Just then, Mr. Paulson leaned against the table and hung his head with his eyes looking at the pencil he was nervously fumbling around in his hands. His foot was tapping uneasily. Then, Mr. Lynn coldly said, "We can't do that. Mr. Gregory died in his sleep last night."

Dave and Mel fell back in their chairs with unbelief as Mr. Lynn continued, "As it turns out, Mr. Gregory had a case of congestive heart failure, which was brought on by sleep apnea.

Our doctors missed this during their examination, and last night as he slept, Mr. Gregory's heart just gave out on him. He was found this morning when we were taking him his breakfast."

"That's awfully convenient!" Mel said with disdain in his voice. "What are you insinuating?" said Mr. Lynn. "Nothing," Mel answered. "It's just that you couldn't have done anything to Brian! After all, he has been missing for twelve months and was declared dead nine months ago!

What's more, there is no evidence that he was ever here. Except for us, of course." Dave and Mel just sat staring, unafraid at Mr. Lynn.

Dave quickly chimed in, "What are you going to do with us? We haven't disappeared or died recently! Quite a few people would actually miss us. And what about the A/V techs Seth and Larry and all the other people who were listening in yesterday.

What if they started hearing rumors of our demise? I'll bet they would all be racing to see who could spill the beans first! However, I'm sure that you will be able to count on your two trustworthy doctors, especially when they are put under the pressure of sitting in front of a Senate Criminal Action hearing."

Mel added, "It seems to me, Mr. Lynn, that by overstepping your authority, you have lost control of this investigation! Something tells me that your superiors will look upon your actions unfavorably!"

Several minutes passed as Mr. Lynn's expression changed from defiance to repentance. Then, in a much more, humble tone he said, "Mr. Gregory really did die in his sleep last night. And no, it was not convenient! I had orders to take him to an institution where we house people like him. I already have very much to answer for. And yes, you are right. I have lost control of this investigation!

Gentlemen, I'm so sorry I put you through this. You are both seasoned agents with excellent records, yet I was willing to destroy you both to achieve my goals. I have been doing this for so long that the right and wrong of what I was doing just got lost somewhere along the way. I am open to any suggestions if you are still willing to help. Mel, what do you think would be the best way to handle this?"

Grasping the opportunity, Mel took things in hand, "The first thing you need to do is to notify your superiors that you have the full audio and video statement that Brian Gregory made just before he died. Furthermore, let them know that

Brian had told us that he would never tell his story again. What's more, that you are sure that he knew he was dying. This will give the recordings the validity of a deathbed confession.

Next, you need to drop the Brian Gregory investigation immediately! It is literally at a dead end and must be pursued no further. Lastly, before they can stop you, release Brian's body to his family. This situation may still get a little messy, but it could get a whole lot worse if pursued. Leaning forward in his seat with his hands folded, looking at the floor, Mr. Lynn nodded in agreement and said, "Yes, Mr. Brooks, you are absolutely right."

Mr. Lynn pulled out a cell phone and started texting. He sent the order to have Brian's body immediately released, and a transport arranged to take him home. Lastly, he texts his superiors, recommending the exact plan of action that Mel had laid out.

When he had finished, he said, "Thank you! This is the first time that I've ever felt good about myself after an investigation. I will notify the family myself in person and try to explain. What are you two going to do now?"

Dave answered, "Well...I'm going to take the rest of the day off to spend time with my family. Tomorrow I will go back to work and take things as they come!" "Sounds good to me," Mel said in agreement.

Mr. Paulson, who had been quiet all this time, reminded them, "Tomorrow, there will be questions from both of your agencies. What will you tell them?" Dave and Mel looked at each other, then smiled at the two HSA agents. Then Mel said, "We will only tell them, as much as they are willing to hear!"

"God help us all!" Mr. Lynn declared, "We are going to need it." The four men felt their burdens lifted, even as their hearts were grieving for Brian, the one who had started all this. They left the bunker with a new outlook on life, with a new worldview, and they were at peace with their choice.

THE REST OF THE STORY

A few years after Brian's time at the bunker, the sixth millennium was coming to a climactic close. Wars were on every continent, as the new One World Government was attempting to enforce their new laws and were subjecting the so-called dissidents to death and imprisonment. The world, therefore, had been reduced to just two camps, the Globalist and The People of God.

By this time, the Noaans had been extinguished altogether. Through the use of underground neutron radiation devices, the Globalists could destroy all life in the underground caverns without collapsing them.

The Movement, now calling themselves the Globalist, were planning to move into the environments to protect themselves from the calamities occurring on the surface. They blamed those they referred to as TPOGs, 'The People of God', for their failure to save the world from the catastrophes.

In times past, this distraction was used to shift the responsibility for the death and destruction that plagued a population away from those in power. Since the days long before Nero, governments have blamed god's people for the troubles which had come upon their nations. This time, however, it was the whole world!

Therefore, the TPOGs retreated to the last remaining wildernesses and mountain sanctuaries, with the Globalists hounding their every step. Even so, in a last-ditch effort, some stayed behind, knowing they had the only solution for the dying world! They met with unimaginable persecution for the hope that just one would listen. The TPOGs knew that time was running out, and all this was going to end!

Just a few years before, many of God's people had attempted to store up food, water, clothing, and even weapons in preparation for the last days. However, it was all in vain; there was no way to prepare for what was happening other than sharing the Message. Everything in this world was going to be destroyed. Except for those who put their faith in God's grace by accepting His salvation through His Son, Jesus Christ!

The enemy had instilled fear into the hearts of the masses, even those who professed to be Christian but were trusting in their own works to save them. This was the time when you saved your life by laying down your life, and by saving your life, you lost it forever! The Bible tells us, it is appointed for all men to die once; only the lost will see the second death. This is why the TPOGs tried so desperately to warn all those who were lost.

The TPOG's Message was that we are all sinners, and there is nothing we can do apart from God's grace to be saved. We are all wretched, miserable, poor, blind, and naked. Without Jesus' righteousness to clothe us, we cannot stand before God! Even so, few listened, and even fewer were willing to believe.

The remaining believers found themselves under assault spiritually as well. Knowing that he was running out of time, the enemy pounded their senses with guilt, doubt, and condemnation. He told them they had put their faith in a fairy tale, and it was not enough to save them. Insanity is the only way to describe his state of mind, as he realized the fear of facing his creator and God in the judgment!

In the meantime, the Globalist, fully knowing that the earth's last days were at hand, refused to relent in their tireless persecution of the TPOGs. In mindless disobedience to God, the Globalists committed all of their resources to their destruction.

However, just before they achieved this Final Goal, the entire universe was shaken! A thundering voice proclaimed, "It is done! All who are Clean, are Clean, All who are Unclean, shall remain Unclean!"

The Earth shook as if it was trying to resist God's will by attempting to hold back His treasure. Nevertheless, as the lost people desperately ran to hide themselves from Him, the ground erupted, and the seas exploded! God's treasure, the saved who had died throughout all ages, burst forth and faster than the speed of light, found themselves in His presence, above the sky...

...Suddenly standing, looking at his hands and feeling the blood pulse through his veins, Brian wonders. Is this it? Am I really here? Will God accept me? As he becomes aware of the multitude of people and angels around him, he realizes that he can feel their emotions and understand their thoughts. When he and the others started making eye contact, a singular thought suddenly flashed in their minds...Jesus!

Then Brian, and all the others, as if they were one, pivoted and saw Him! The first thing Brian noticed was that He was smiling, with a Joy that only He could have. As He radiated Love from Himself, all their guilt melted away, and He replaced their fears with His own indescribable Joy! The people of God actually started glowing!

However, the light shone brightest around the children!

There were countless numbers of children who had died throughout the ages. All those who had not lived to reach the age of choice! Babies were carried to their mother's arms by the awestruck angels. The little ones, whose parents had chosen not to come, became the children of those who had none of their own. Finally, the light grew brighter than the sun, as many women felt life returning to their womb, and they burst out in tears of joy! This was the beginning of the Healing of the Nations.

At that moment, with just a glance, Yahshua sent His angels to recover the remainder of His treasure. His remaining treasure were those who had not perished in the persecution. The angels are amazing creatures, more beautiful than anything on earth. They shot straight upwards over the heads of the saints and, with hyper-precision, raced downward towards the earth like bolts of lightning.

In less than a heartbeat, the surviving saints of God were standing among us. As they were figuring out the same thing we had only seconds earlier, their Joy became complete as well. God's work was almost done. Finally, He bestowed his greatest gift on His children…Eternal Life!

The children of God, who were now made whole, broke out in a song. A song that God had put into their hearts at creation. A song He had waited, all this time to hear. As the song went up, rows and rows of angels encircled them. The angels could not sing this song themselves, so they folded their wings and bowed their heads in worship to God for His amazing power and Love. Because, what God had started so long ago, He had now finished.

Brian thought there was no way for his joy to increase because his family, friends, Mel and Dave, Mr. Paulson, and Mr. Lynn were all standing beside him! Even two ex-scientists were standing there, with arms raised in praise, for the undeserved Grace of God.

All of a sudden, Brian saw the Noaans, with the red hem of the martyrs on their robes. And there was Sada, smiling as if to say, I told you so! Brian ran over, grabbed him, and gave him a huge bear hug. Life was at last complete because God is Love!

Brian remembered back when he had visited some of the churches, where he heard preachers saying that God was angry and was coming to destroy the wicked! However, this was not so! He came to save the wicked from their sin, the same sin that would eventually kill the world. This was a rescue mission!

God gave them the Word, the evidence of their faith and Himself to die. Thus, He paid the price for their redemption! As a result, all those who came to Him in faith, He made clean; those who did not did so by their own choice. "In Him was life, and the life was the light of men. And the light shineth in darkness; and the darkness comprehended it not."

Far below, the world grew cold, dark, and lifeless, except for the one who had rebelled in Heaven, the one condemned to wander the earth alone until the day of his final judgment.

Brian was just beginning to understand when suddenly, they all found themselves standing on the sea of glass in the Kingdom itself! The only thing Sada could say was, "WOW!" Brian smiled and told him, "What do you know...

I Am Bigfoot

gbmsound.com

www.ingramcontent.com/pod-product-compliance
Lightning Source LLC
Chambersburg PA
CBHW070533130626
46555CB00003B/1404